More **Dark Man** book

First series

The Dark Fire of Doom	978-184167-417-9
Destiny in the Dark	978-184167-422-3
The Dark Never Hides	978-184167-419-3
The Face in the Dark Mirror	978-184167-411-7
Fear in the Dark	978-184167-412-4
Escape from the Dark	978-184167-416-2
Danger in the Dark	978-184167-415-5
The Dark Dreams of Hell	978-184167-418-6
The Dark Side of Magic	978-184167-414-8
The Dark Glass	978-184167-421-6
The Dark Waters of Time	978-184167-413-1
The Shadow in the Dark	978-184167-420-9

Second series

The Dark Candle	978-184167-603-6
The Dark Machine	978-184167-601-2
The Dark Words	978-184167-602-9
Dying for the Dark	978-184167-604-3
Killer in the Dark	978-184167-605-0
The Day is Dark	978-184167-606-7
The Dark River	978-184167-745-3
The Bridge of Dark Tears	978-184167-746-0
The Past is Dark	978-184167-747-7
Playing the Dark Game	978-184167-748-4
The Dark Music	184167-749-1
The Dark Gard	84167-750-7

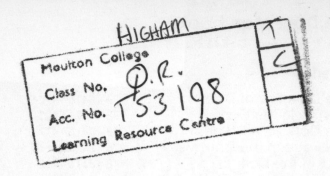

Dark Man

The Dark Glass
by Peter Lancett
illustrated by Jan Pedroietta

Published by Ransom Publishing Ltd.
Radley House, 8 St. Cross Road, Winchester, Hampshire
SO23 9HX
www.ransom.co.uk

ISBN   978 184167 421 6
First published in 2006
Reprinted 2008, 2012

Dark Man

The Dark Glass

by Peter Lancett

illustrated by Jan Pedroietta

Ransom

Chapter One:
The Girl

In a dirty room in the bad part of the city, there is a bed.

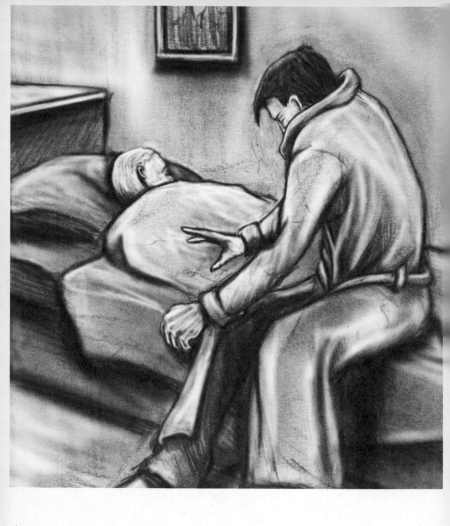

The Dark Man sits by the bed.

A girl, covered with a blanket, lies there.

The girl is dying, and not even magic
can save her.

"The Dark Glass can help you see the Golden Cup," she says softly.

"You must take it from them."

The Dark Man nods as she tells him where to find the Dark Glass.

The girl falls back onto her pillow and sleeps.

Chapter Two:
The Busy Streets

In the smart part of the city, the sun is shining.

The Dark Man walks the busy streets.

No one seems to see him, he is just one person among many.

He does not like it here, and he does not like the light.

People smile, and all things are new and clean and shiny.

This is not his world.

But this is where the Shadow Masters
hold the Dark Glass.

Chapter Three:
In the Office

Steps lead up to the glass doors of an office block.

The Dark Man enters.

He takes the lift to the top floor, to an office high above the city.

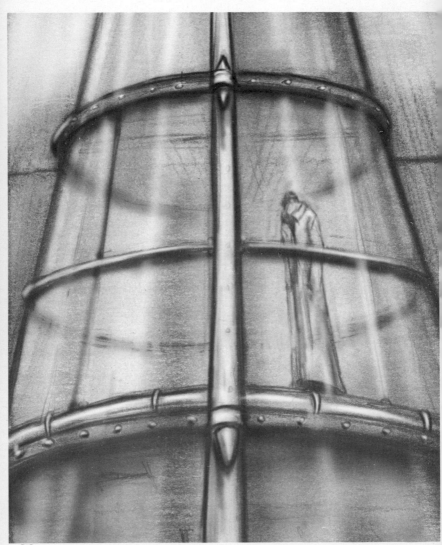

A man sits behind a desk.

He sees the Dark Man and rises from his seat.

"I know what you are after," the man says.

"Find it if you can."

"You will show me where it is," the Dark Man replies.

The man shakes his head and says, "Make me."

The Dark Man steps towards the desk.

The man behind it no longer smiles.

On the desk, the Dark Man notices a large, flat stone.

The man reaches out to pick up the stone, but the Dark Man is faster.

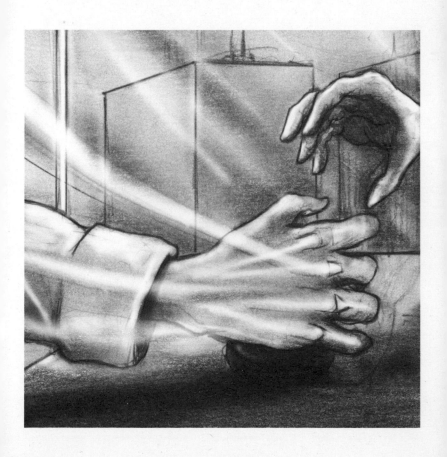

"I said that you would show me," the Dark Man says.

The man screams and rushes at the Dark Man.

The Dark Man pushes him back and he smashes through a window.

The man seems to hang in the air, then he is gone.

The window is unbroken.

The man had been a demon.

Chapter Four:
The Dark Glass

The Dark Man looks at the stone.

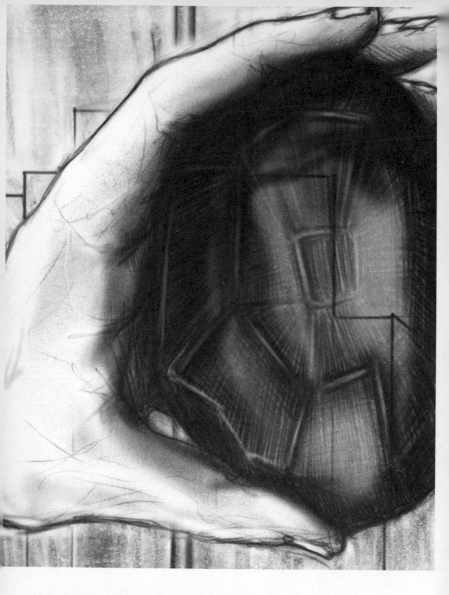

It becomes very smooth.

It is dark but he can see through it.

It is the Dark Glass.

He puts it in his pocket and feels it
become stone again.

The girl will be happy, he thinks.

But he knows he will never see her again.

The author

photograph: Rachel Ottewill

Peter Lancett used to work in the movies. Then he worked in the city. Now he writes horror stories for a living. "It beats having a proper job," he says.